# Willow-Mia Pig

## 1 in 100 Million

by Nancy A. Bolanis · illustrated by Donna Secour

NANCY ANN PRODUCTIONS, LLC • NEWTON, MA

*This book is dedicated to the Humane Society of the United States under the wonderful leadership of Wayne Pacelle, and to Debra White, founder of Winslow Farm Animal Sanctuary, "who see the little eyes in the cages." My sincere thanks and appreciation go to both of them for their ongoing support regarding the humane treatment of animals.*

Mary Mahony, Editor
Susan A. Pasternack, Copy Editor
Illustrations by Donna Secour
Cover and design by Blue Iris Design
Printed by Bang Printing, Brainerd, MN

Fiction. Juvenile.
Library of Congress Control Number: 2013916149
ISBN: 978-0-615-79112-8

$\mathcal{H}$ello there! My name is Willow-Mia Pig and this is my tale. And I don't mean the squiggly one at the end of my backside. I mean tale as in a story.

One cold October morning I was snuggled up against my mama, along with my brothers and sisters, drinking her warm milk and enjoying the comfort of our nice warm barn. All of a sudden two big cold hands came down and grabbed me by my little pink belly. Up in the air I went, with my mama squealing and crying below. Then the man snatched my mama and shoved her into a cage. She shrieked in pain as her legs gave out. I didn't know that this would be the last time I ever saw my mama.

Then SNAP! OUCH! Those same hands grabbed me again and the man punched a thick, red tag into my tiny ear, carelessly taking off part of my ear as he did this. I was number 228 and boy did that number hurt. Then those hands pushed me and my brothers and sisters into a wooden crate. We felt this big thump as we were tossed into the back of a truck. The thump soon became a bumpity, bump, bump while we traveled down the country road out onto a big highway.

Then bumpity, bump, bump turned into bangity, bang, bang, thump, thump, and screech. The truck came to a very quick stop, and my brothers and sisters and I tumbled over each other. Not just us, but the whole truck was tilted to one side. That's when I spotted the cracks and then a hole in two of the boards of our crate.

Mama always taught us to do whatever we needed to be safe. I could hear her telling us, "jump, jump." I knew that the only way we would be safe was to do just that. I told my brothers and sisters what Mama would want us to do. I begged them to jump, too, but I could see they were too scared to join me.

The truck began inching forward and I knew this was my last chance to get free. I took in a deep breath, let it all out, and with all my might, squeezed through the broken boards. I could not believe my eyes. I was outside the crate! Then the truck lurched forward and out the back I flew into the air, spinning and tumbling. I landed in a whole lot of mud. SPLASH! SPLAT! OUCH! Every inch of my little pink body hurt. My ear burned more than ever. I missed Mama and I was so scared that I lay down and sobbed myself to sleep under a willow tree.

When I woke up, it was dark. I had no idea where I was or how I got there. I could hear this very loud "whoosh, whoosh, whoosh," as an endless stream of cars with bright white lights rushed by. I found myself in a muddy ditch right next to a busy highway. Before too long the sun came up, and I could hear my tummy grumbling for food. I chomped on some green grass since it was the only thing there except dirt and sticks.

*I* spent my whole day listening to the whoosh of the cars. Soon the sun set and it was nighttime again. I missed my mama more than ever and I was worried about my brothers and sisters. It was freezing cold and the wind only made it worse. I huddled back in the ditch under my willow tree as best I could, and once again, I cried myself to sleep.

When morning came, I followed the whoosh, whoosh of the cars and dragged my tired, hungry body back up from the ditch to the highway. The cars came so close that I decided to go back down into the ditch again. For I don't know how long, I did the same thing each day, still only finding grass to eat. Often when I went up the hill, a car would slow down as it passed by and I saw the people in the car staring at me. Some even opened their windows and I could hear them saying, "Oh, you poor little piggy. You must be lost. Don't worry, we'll get some help." Then I would get scared and run back down to the safety of my ditch.

I couldn't stop thinking about Mama and how much I missed snuggling up to her warm body. Even though I was safe from bars and crates, I wondered if I would ever feel loved and wanted again.

*I* don't know exactly how long my life went on like this, but one day a car with a flashy red light pulled over to the side of the highway near my ditch. I saw the letters P-O-L-I-C-E on the side of the car. A man in fancy blue clothes got out and stood there for a minute chatting on a phone. Then he got a cage from the back of his car, walked slowly toward me, and kept calling out, "Here piggy, piggy. Nice piggy, piggy." When he saw me, he placed the metal cage on the grass. Then he put a big gooey cinnamon bun dripping with wonderful brown sugary syrup into the back of the cage. My snout went up and sniffed the yummy smell. My belly was telling me to go for it, but my mind was reminding me of Mama's sad eyes. I curled my body up and tried to hide in the grass.

Soon the man walked back to his car and drove away, leaving the cage behind. Then I crept over to the back of the cage and pressed my snout against the bars. I wanted to see if there was any way I could get a little taste of the cinnamon bun. Tears poured down my cheeks when I realized that I couldn't get at the bun without going into the cage and becoming trapped like Mama, so I stayed safe outside. Like I had done many nights before, I cried myself to sleep.

$\mathcal{T}$he very next morning, I awoke to the sound of a man slamming a door as he got out of a bright red-and-green van that he had parked not far from my ditch. I squealed in fear and jumped into the air, but I was too weak to run. I tried to get to the back of my ditch, but in my panic I ran snout first into a section of fence that separated the highway from the hill above my ditch. Suddenly I felt a big net being tossed over my head. I tried to break free but my hooves got caught.

The man then put me into a cage, put the cage into the van, and slammed the door shut. I sat in the dark shaking with fear. And then I heard that same bang, bang, thump, thump. But just when I thought I was trapped forever, the van door opened and I saw the man looking at me with a warm smile. For a minute I almost felt safe again. He carried me and my cage into a big building. Once we were inside, he opened the door of the cage and wagged a biscuit right in front of my snout. I started to make my way toward the tasty treat, which he had tossed into a soft bed nearby. I snatched it from the bed as fast as I could. I was so happy to be eating real food again. While I was crunching on the biscuit, the man carefully cut off the tag from my ear. He gently wiped my ear with lotion and told me how sorry he was that part of it was missing. He pulled a bunch of itchy ticks from my neck and gently washed my sores. Then he gave me a soft stuffed toy and patted my neck. The last thing I heard him say as I drifted off to sleep was, "Welcome to the dog shelter, Willow-Mia Pig."

5

When I awoke the next day, I found myself in a big box called a kennel. It may sound like a cage but it wasn't, really. It had one clear see-through wall with a small round hole near the bottom. I could put my snout up to the hole and sniff, but my snout was too big to poke through.

Then I realized that three young women were staring at me. They all had on the same red shirts. I guess it was their special work shirt. I think they really liked me, because they pressed their noses against the clear wall to get a better look, and pretty soon we were pressing nose to snout! They brought me a blanket, some water, and a bowl of great food. As I squealed with joy, I could hear this grrrr, grrrr, woof, woof that soon became a very loud BARK! Yikes, there were two nostrils sniffing my kennel. I followed them with my eyes and I could see this big brown dog staring at me. What kind of shelter was this? Where were the pigs?

I was relieved when the dog finally lay down. When I was sure he was asleep, I explored my new bed and water dish. I backed into the rear wall of my kennel and a small door swung open. Startled, I jumped, and then I watched it move back and forth. I thought I saw sunlight! Can this really be? Am I allowed to just walk through that opening and go outside? I was a little scared that it might be a trick, but I decided to take a chance. I let out a really big grunt and pushed my way through with all my might. I then realized that my kennel had two parts, an inside and an outside. Outside, I felt the sun and the crisp breeze on my sore body. I felt so happy and safe. Well, almost safe.

$O$ut of the corner of my eye, I noticed a big black dog pouncing around the yard with one of the young women. I crouched down, hoping they wouldn't notice me. Pretty soon I saw a bunch of dogs playing in the yard and having fun. I really wanted to join them, but I wasn't sure how they felt about pigs.

Days passed, and I would watch the dogs play. In time, I even had favorites: Sheba, the German shepherd, was the best catcher on the fly. Doc, the Great Dane mix, zigzagged so quickly as he ran that he looked like a big blurry moving shadow. Shadow seemed a better name for him than Doc.

Many people would come and visit with the dogs and often someone would take one home. It was always a great day when that happened. I watched the lucky dog being led out of the kennel with her new owners. I wondered if anyone would ever want to take me home. Sure, lots of people noticed me as they passed by my kennel. Most of them said nice things, but I could tell they were surprised to see a pig in a dog shelter. A few of them were very loud and hurtful, calling me names. "What's that scrawny pig doing in there," I would hear them say. "No one is ever going to want to adopt a pig." Sometimes I would go over to my "sniff hole" and greet them with a snortle, but they would just laugh even louder and walk over to the dogs. I can play, too. Why doesn't anyone ever want to throw a ball for me and give me some attention?

*T*hen one day, when I had just about lost all hope for a better life, a lady appeared at my kennel. She told me her name was Mollie. She had gray-blue eyes that matched her old gray-blue jeans, and dark blonde hair, just like a pony's tail. I could tell that she looked at me differently, not like all the others. She stepped right into my kennel and sat down on a red milk crate, and said, "Wil…low-Meeeee…aaaa, you sure are a sweeeeeeetheart. You my girl? Hmmm? You are sooooo cute. You my girl? Oh, yes you are!"

I just didn't know what to make of this Mollie. She smelled really good and had a soft smile and even softer eyes. She looked right at me and I looked right back at her. My heart melted as I flapped my ears this way and that. I wanted to sing, and dance, and do somersaults! I was happier than I had been in a very long time.

I strolled around my kennel, looking partly away from Mollie; I just knew I wanted to circle in closer and closer. When I finally brushed against her jeans, she cooed softly, "Willow-Mia. Sweetheart. You my girl?" I snortled back, "Yes, I am. Yes, I am your girl." Then I gently popped her with my snout a few times and took a taste of her shoe. She laughed, "Ouch! No, no, Willow-Mia," but we both knew I hadn't really hurt her. She kept patting my head and my back, and I felt wonderfully safe and loved, just like when Mama did those things. I even let Mollie touch my right ear, the one without the tip, which now curled over a bit.

$\mathcal{M}$ollie came in most days and sat on her red crate, giving me lots of pats and attention. She even brought me toys to nibble on. I soon learned that when Mollie said "down," it meant that I would get a good belly rub. I would flop down on my front legs and back legs and then roll over on my back next to her.

Mollie also brought me great food treats, like grapes and watermelon and yummy biscuits. One day she even came with a tray of food, like a feast, including a large white egg that she put right in front of my snout. I took a quick sniff and then chomp, chomp, chomp into my belly it went! Some of the yellow yoke squirted out of my mouth and dripped onto the ground. As I went to lick up all of the yoke bits from the floor, I tossed my head up, rolling my eyes back in sheer joy.

One day Mollie brought someone with her. She said he was a dog trainer. He was holding the red harness that I had worn once before. At first I was afraid, but then Mollie told me I would be OK. As I took a treat from Mollie's hand, the trainer slipped the harness over my shoulders and clipped the buckle. Then he made the door of my kennel fly open and in a flash I was out! We strolled right out front and said hello to everyone, and then went out into the kennel yard. All the shelter workers seemed happy to see me. The trainer then placed a rainbow-colored hoop in front of me. I strutted through the hoop and out the other side. Mollie beamed with pride at my trick.

$\mathcal{N}$ext Mollie took me out to the yard where the dogs played. Because I still felt a little frightened of the dogs, it had been a while since I had gone outside and felt grass and dirt under my feet. Sweet grass! Soft dirt! I felt my insides just exploding with joy. The yard was empty and Mollie let me run from one end to the other. Oh how Mollie laughed at my show! I rooted a tunnel here and a tunnel there. You would be amazed at what I can find when I root around, kind of like spying a hidden treasure.

*I* flipped onto my side into that precious dirt, red harness and all, wiggling this way and that. I danced for the whole world to see, and most especially, I danced for me. For the grand finale, I got on my elbows (I have elbows just like you), and I danced right through my tunnels. Now it was Mollie who was squealing with delight!

When night came, I fell into a peaceful sleep. I felt as if my insides were glowing in the dark, as if someone had climbed in and put a string of twinkling lights inside my little body. I was in pig heaven.

$\mathcal{E}$ach day I would hear the high pitched "Willlll…lllow-Meeeee…aaaaa, come see Mollie," and I would dance over to her, snortling and grunting with joy. Sometimes I got so excited that I even trumpeted! Always, always Mollie would cry out, "You are soooo cute, Willow-Mia. You my girl? Yes, you are. Yes, you are!" That's when I flapped my ears so hard that I air-lifted myself right off the floor. I uncurled my tail and waved it like a flag. Mollie gave me a tasty biscuit. Chomp! Chomp! Smack! Smack! Mollie and me! Mollie and me! Oh, how I loved my Mollie, and I knew she loved me.

Mollie continued to come every day and she always brought me good treats. I would bang my snout on my sniff hole each time I saw her, just aching to schnoodle up next to her. Sometimes I pressed my nose so hard against the sniff hole that I made a little mark on the top of my nose, right at 12 o'clock. But sometimes, when I looked at Mollie, I saw that her gray-blue eyes looked red and I wondered if she had been crying. That's when I would start to feel scared again.

One day Mollie came and put her face up against my kennel and whispered, "Willow-Mia, we think we have found a home for you. It is a very special place called an animal sanctuary farm. It gives animals a wonderful home, where they are loved and cared for by a very special lady named Debra. Even though Debra says she doesn't have room for you right now, she has invited me to visit her farm. A woman named Alexis is going to go with me. Her job is to help find homes for animals like you that have no place to live.

"Oh, Willow-Mia, Debra's farm will be so perfect for you. The animals come from all over and many of them have had difficult journeys, just like you. On the farm, they are safe and well cared for and never have to be afraid of anyone ever again. Debra is very interested in your story. She laughed when I told her how you eat your food, smack, smack, smacking your lips and popping your snout."

*W*ell, I had heard enough! My insides were in knots. I crawled under my blanket and coiled up my tail. I just wanted to be alone. There was really no place for pigs like me. Even when I thought I was loved and wanted again, something always went wrong. I remembered hearing a visitor once say, "She is the luckiest pig around. Maybe she is 1 in 100 million, since most pigs end up on a dinner plate!" At the time, I thought she was being really mean, but I think she was probably right. I was just a hopeless, sad, lonely pig that didn't even have a place to call home.

Mollie could see how upset I was. "Hey you. You still my girl? Hmm. Aww, come on. Yes, you know you're my girl, don't you?" This time, I didn't snortle back. No, not this time. I just stayed buried under my blanket. I should have known that this was just a trick and that being safe and comfortable would soon come to an end.

Then I heard Mollie say, "I'm here for you, Willow-Mia Pig. I'll just have to *pig on* without you!"

After Mollie left, I climbed out from under my bed and stared at my reflection in the clear wall of my kennel. I looked at my big flappy ears. I studied myself from my snout to my lightly spotted pink skin, to my short, thin, white hair, down to my legs, and finally, my hooves. I wondered why a nice pig like me had to have such a hard life. Then I squealed loudly, snortling so hard that I tumbled right over on my side. That is what "pig on" really meant. Once a pig, always a pig; there was no way I could turn the pig off in me. Yet I knew that Mollie loved me just the same.

Fall came and went and then it was winter. Brrr. It was very cold outside, and I was still in the dog shelter growing bigger and bigger and bigger. That is when I was moved into a bigger space where I could move around more easily. My new home was a maroon shed, filled with hay. When I played outside, they often wrapped me in a red waterproof doggie jacket with snazzy gray stripes to keep me snuggly and warm. At night, I tunneled into the hay. Sometimes, Mollie came by with treats, but she didn't stay very long. The air was too cold and raw. I couldn't watch the dogs when they played in the yard anymore because my shed was in a different place. That made me lonely and sad. Thank goodness for the two goats at the shelter that shared the back fence line with me.

$\mathcal{B}$y this time, I wasn't a little piggy anymore. I would soon weigh 200 pounds. All I wanted was to find a real home or maybe a real home would come find me. Why couldn't I be as lucky as the dogs in the kennel and get adopted?

Then something amazing happened. It was just an ordinary day at the dog shelter. I woke up and did my usual morning routine: I gruntled, snortled, and scratched, and when I finally peeked out of my shed, I saw Mollie leaning against the fence. But on this day Mollie was not alone. There was a lady standing next to her. Was it Debra from the farm? I felt a connection to her right away. Was it her warm smile? Was it her blue jeans, her farm hat, her barn coat? I could feel my tummy getting those knots in it again. What if Debra doesn't like me the way Mollie does? I wanted her to like me and I knew just how to do that!

I trotted over to where they were and stood at attention with my head up. I flapped my ears two or three times to be sure Debra noticed me. "Hello! Hello, Willow-Mia Pig," Debra said. "You are such a precious, sweet pig and I love how you flapped your ears at me." Then she bent down and looked at me, and we were eye to eye, knee to knee. That's when I heard her say, "Willow-Mia Pig, I have made a place for you at my farm and I think you will really like it there."

For a minute I thought I was dreaming. Did I just hear her say that she had made a place for me at her farm? She started telling me about her farm and how I would fit in with all the other animals. I realized that it was not a dream at all. Finally, I was going to my forever home. I started squealing loudly, spinning and dancing with joy! I wanted to hear those words over and over again. My forever home!

And so, on that bitter-cold February day, after months of good care at the dog shelter, I was about to go to my forever home.

After they put my red harness on, I proudly marched up the ramp into the back of Debra's special truck. This ride would be a lot different from the last one. This time there was no crate, and I rested comfortably, knowing that I was on my way to this very special place.

Before long I arrived at the most magical place on earth. As I strolled down the truck ramp, I was greeted by sheep, goats, ducks, ponies, llamas, alpacas, dogs, and cats. Oh yes, there were even pigs, including Mr. Waterbelly, an 800-pound brown Tamworth who had the biggest snout and ears I had ever seen in my whole pig life.

It was all so exciting! Finally, I was someone, I was welcome, and I knew I was really home. From the yard of the farm I saw this wonderful little barn, a special shed filled with soft hay. The front door was made of clear plastic flaps. I could go in and out whenever I wanted. There were no bars and no cages. Debra had placed a sign on the top of the door that read, Willow-Mia Pig. I had my own special spot, my forever home. My eyes filled with so many tears that my ears could not wipe them off my piggy cheeks fast enough, and their salty taste was making me hungry. Debra bent down and put out a bowl of the best "sow chow" I had ever tasted.

*A*s the sun began to set, I strolled around the farm. It was very different from the place where I had lived with Mama. Here I knew that I would always be safe and loved and wanted. I saw that the barns and other buildings were all framed with twinkling lights, the same twinkling lights that had made me feel as if my whole body was aglow when I had first met Mollie.

As I watched the ducks quacking and splashing in the water, the goats playing with a pail, the ponies sauntering about, and Mr. Waterbelly having a wonderful time rooting away, I knew that my worries were finally over. I would never be a pig on a plate. I was in a place where everyone shared and everyone cared about each other. Best of all, they were all my friends.

I love living on the farm. Mollie comes by and visits me whenever she can. As soon as she gets out of her car I hear, "Will…low-Meeeee…aaaa. You are so cute! You my girl? Yes, you are." That's when I trot over and get my warm rubs and tasty treats. I love Mollie and now I also love Debra. Most of all, I love my new home. Sometimes at night, when I am all cuddled up in the hay, I think about how lucky I am. Even though Debra's farm had no room, she worked hard to make a place for me and to care about me, me, little old me, Willow-Mia Pig.

So this is my tale, Willow-Mia Pig. I am 1 in 100 million.

This story is just one example of an animal that was mistreated. Luckily for Willow-Mia Pig, she was found by people who truly cared about her safety and well-being and nurtured her back to health. Although you may not know it, pigs are very clean animals. They lie in the mud to keep cool. Pigs always make sure that the area they sleep in is very clean and the same is true of young piglets. They are intelligent, caring, and very social animals that love people, and it is easy to become as attached to a pig as you would to any other animal. Their favorite thing is to root in the soil for goodies that give them the vitamins and minerals they need to stay healthy and grow. And oh, my, do they grow and grow and grow, just like Mr. Waterbelly. At this writing, little Willow-Mia Pig is a very big 200 pounds, and she still flirts and snortles with anyone who comes to visit her.

Sadly, most pigs are not treated well today because of something called factory farming. The young piglets are removed from their mothers too soon, and put into crates, just like what happened to Willow-Mia Pig, and brought to factory farms. There, they are shoved into small, overcrowded spaces that are poorly kept, never to have the sunshine on their backs or to root in the dirt again. They are given the wrong foods to fatten them up for slaughter more quickly, and their lives are cut short far too soon. This is the fate of more than 100 million pigs each year in the United States alone.

We hope you now have a better understanding of how hard it is to be a pig in today's world. Perhaps you also have a wonderful appreciation of how important it is to treat your own pets with kindness, just as you would want someone to treat you. If you don't have a pet and are thinking of getting one, there are many wonderful animals just waiting for a second chance. Do consider giving them one.

Thanks to caring people like Debra White, the founder of Winslow Farm Animal Sanctuary, abandoned and mistreated animals like Willow-Mia Pig have that second chance at life. There, along with more than 200 other once-abandoned and abused animals, they roam freely and feel the sun on their faces and the wind on their backs. Debra's loving care and ongoing mission to rescue these animals is a fine example of how we should be treating our animals. Learn from her, and if you have time, take a field trip to Norton, Massachusetts, and visit her farm. Make sure you introduce yourself to Willow-Mia Pig and tell her how much you enjoyed her story. I am sure she will "snortle" with delight!

# ABOUT THE AUTHOR

Nancy A. Bolanis grew up in Stamford and New Caanan, Connecticut, and as a young girl had a deep love of animals. Her caring spirit led her to the medical profession, and she is currently in private practice at a hospital in a suburb outside of Boston, Massachusetts. In spite of her very busy practice, her interest in the welfare of animals has never waned. Today, Nancy continues to support a number of initiatives such as factory-farming bills that focus on the more humane treatment of animals. She is a strong supporter of the Humane Society of the United States as well as Winslow Farm Animal Sanctuary.

Like many who so generously answer pleas that come across local television stations, Nancy responded to a news broadcast about a pig, now Willow-Mia Pig, who was found on the side of Route 495 in Massachusetts in 2012. After seeing Willow-Mia Pig through to a safe haven, Nancy was inspired by Willow-Mia Pig's journey and decided to share it with children. Her goal is to ensure that both children and adults become more aware of the importance of treating animals with love and kindness. Nancy continues to surround herself with others who "dare to care," and her contagious enthusiasm has created a tremendous groundswell of support to see that farms are held accountable to certain standards when caring for animals. Nancy hopes that her story will also inspire you to "dare to care."

Mollie's real name is Nancy, the author of this story. She chose to use the name Mollie in the story as it is the name of her dog. As you can see in this photo, a big part of Nancy's life is her love of animals, whether it be a pig named Willow-Mia, or a dog named Mollie.

Nancy Ann and Willow-Mia Pig
The woman who "dared to care."

Mollie's real name is Nancy, the author of this story. She chose to use the name Mollie in the story since it is the name of her dog. A big part of Nancy's life is her love of animals, whether it be a pig named Willow-Mia, or her dog named Mollie.

If you would like to support Winslow Farm Animal Sanctuary, go to: www.winslowfarm.com.

If you would like to support the Humane Society of the United States, go to: www.humanesociety.org.

All donations are very much appreciated. We hope that everyone will "dare to care."

Willow-Mia Pig thanks you.

Snortle, snortle.